Baby Talk

written by **FRED HIATT** · illustrated by **MARK GRAHAM**

MARGARET K. MCELDERRY BOOKS

By the same author and illustrator:

If I Were Queen of the World

Margaret K. McElderry Books
An imprint of Simon & Schuster Children's Publishing Division
1230 Avenue of the Americas
New York, NY 10020

Book design by Angela Carlino
The text of this book was set in Janson Text.
The illustrations were rendered in oil paint.

Printed in Hong Kong
First Edition
10 9 8 7 6 5 4 3 2 1
Library of Congress Cataloging-in-Publication Data
Hiatt, Fred.
Baby talk / by Fred Hiatt ; illustrated by Mark Graham.—1st ed.
p.   cm.
Summary: Joey finds that he can connect with his new baby brother by speaking his own special language with him.
ISBN 0-689-82146-8
[1. Babies—Fiction. 2. Brothers—Fiction.] I. Graham, Mark, 1952- ill. II. Title.
PZ7.H495Bab   1999   [E]—dc21   97-50550

To Joe and Nathaniel, and Jon, with love
—F. H.

For Josh
—M. G.

"WAAH!" Joey's new baby brother wailed.
Joey covered his ears.
"It's okay," Joey's mother said. "He's just telling us that he's hungry."

"Would you like to try giving him a bottle?"
"No, thank you," Joey said. "You can feed him."

"WAAH! WAAH!" the baby cried again.
"It's okay," said Joey's big sister. "He's saying he needs
a dry diaper."

"Would you like to change him?" Joey's sister asked.
"I don't think so," Joey said. "I'll just watch."

"WAAH! WAAH! WAAH!"

"It's okay," said Joey's father. "He's tired. He's telling us he needs a nap."

"Want to try rocking him to sleep?" Joey's father asked.
"Oh, no," Joey said. "I think you'd better do that."

One day, Joey's baby brother surprised everyone. "Agoo," he said.
"Now what's he saying?" Joey asked.
"You should know," his grandmother said. "He's learning baby talk. You spoke baby talk not so long ago."

Joey tried to remember. But he still couldn't understand.

"Ada," Joey's baby brother said.

"Mom?" Joey said. "Do you know what he's saying?"

"Try talking back," his mom suggested.

"Ageek," said Joey's baby brother.
"Ageek!" answered Joey.
"Ada agoo!" his baby brother said.
"Agoo ada!" said Joey.

"Mom!" Joey called. "He smiled at me!"
"I guess you're speaking his language," said Joey's mom.

After that, Joey and his baby brother talked all the time.
They talked in the car.
"La ga goo!" said Joey's baby brother.
"La ga goo ga!" Joey answered.

They talked on the way to the playground.
"Ba ba!" said Joey's baby brother.
"Ba ba goo!" Joey replied.

They chatted in the supermarket.
"Da fa fa foo?" Joey's baby brother asked.
"Fa foo fa," Joey answered.

They even talked in the tub.
"Doo da!" Joey's baby brother said.
"Da doo da!" Joey agreed.

"What are you two talking about?" Joey's big sister asked one day.
"Ummm . . ." said Joey.
"Sometimes it's hard to translate," said Joey's mom.
"That's true," Joey said.

After a while, Joey thought he understood pretty well.

"A la lee," his baby brother said.

"He wants to play peekaboo," Joey told his mother. "Like this."

"Ta ta ta ta!" Joey's baby brother said.

"That means he wants me to sing to him," Joey told his father.

"I'll show you."

"Goo ba da ba," Joey's baby brother said.

"That's an easy one," Joey told his sister. "He wants me to read him a book."

"AGAGOO!" said Joey's baby brother.

"Now what's he saying?" Joey's grandmother asked.

"It's okay," Joey said. "He's saying he loves his big brother. Right, Baby?"

"A ga goo," Joey's baby brother said.

"A ga goo da," said Joey.